WELCOME TO THE WORLD
OF
Geronimo Stilton

Published by Sweet Cherry Publishing Limited
Unit 36, Vulcan House,
Vulcan Road,
Leicester, LE5 3EF
United Kingdom

First published in the UK in 2018
2020 edition

4 6 8 10 9 7 5

ISBN: 978-1-78226-370-8

Text by Geronimo Stilton
Art Director: Iacopo Bruno
Graphic Designer: Laura Dal Maso / theWorldofDOT
Original cover illustration by Andrea Da Rold and Andrea Cavallini
Concept of illustration by Roberta Bianchi, produced by Cleo Bianca and Christian Alliprandi with
assistance from Lara Martinelli and Tommasco Valsecchi
Initial and final page illustrations by Roberto Ronchi and Ennio Bufi MAD5, Studio Parlapà and
Andrea Cavallini. Map illustrations by Andrea Da Rold
Cover layout and typography by Elena Distefano
Interior layout and typography by Cecilia Bennett, Rhiannon Izard and Amy Wong
Graphics by Merenguita Gingermouse and Sara Baruffaldi
© 2007 Edizioni Piemme S.p.A., Palazzo Mondadori – Via Mondadori, 1 – 20090 Segrate
© 2018 English edition, Sweet Cherry Publishing
International Rights © Atlantyca S.p.A. – Via Leopardi 8, 20123 Milano, Italy
Translation © 2008, Atlantyca S.p.A.

Original title: *Agente segreto Zero Zero Kappa*
Based on an original idea by Elisabetta Dami

www.geronimostilton.com/uk

www.sweetcherrypublishing.com

Printed and bound in Turkey
T.IO006

Geronimo Stilton

GERONIMO STILTON, SECRET AGENT

Sweet Cherry

A SUSPICIOUS-LOOKING RODENT ...

That morning was just like any other morning. I woke up and smelled the cheese – hot Cheddar, that is. I like to make a whole pot every day.

Then I stuffed my paws into my COMFY CAT-FUR SLIPPERS. I shuffled to the window to check the weather. The forecast was for rain. But when I looked outside, I just saw lots of clouds. Clouds, and a very suspicious-looking rodent with dark sunglasses across the street. **How odd.**

I took a shower and gobbled down my breakfast – melted Cheddar toast. Yum! Then I headed for the station. I was humming one of my **favourite love songs**, "Beady-Eyed Beauty", when I saw him again. That same suspicious-looking rodent with the sunglasses was walking right behind me. **How strange.**

A few minutes later, I arrived at my stop. I scampered out the door. Guess who was right on my tail? You got it. Mr. Dark Sunglasses. **How very odd!**

At last, I reached my office at 17 Swiss Cheese Centre. I couldn't believe it. Mr. Sunglasses had beaten me there. I was starting to get a little **CREEPED OUT**. A chill ran down my fur. What did he want from me? **Why was he following me?**

Part of me was afraid to find out. What if he mistook me for an **escaped con rat**? What if I reminded him of someone he didn't like? What if he hated my tie? I decided there was only one thing left to do. I raced up the stairs to my office and slammed the door. Then I buried my snout in my work.

But when I looked out the window at lunchtime, guess who I saw? **Yep, it was that mouse again!**

He was there when I left the office. He was there when I reached my house. He was there after I **WOLFED DOWN** a super-size three-cheese pizza for dinner.

Finally, I couldn't take it anymore. I just had to find out who that mouse was. With a squeak, I yanked open the door to my house. Then I stuck out my snout and yelled, **"WHO ARE YOU AND WHAT DO YOU WANT FROM ME?"**

WHO ARE YOU AND WHAT DO YOU WANT FROM me?

? Don't You Recognise Me?

Even though I was **SCREAMING** at the top of my lungs, the rodent barely reacted. Instead he calmly took off his sunglasses and smiled. Or was it a smirk?

How strange!

The rodent looked so familiar. Was it the trench coat? Was it the paws in the pockets? Was it the *perfectly groomed* fur?

I touched a paw to my own head. Hmmm ... my fur was getting a little long. I made a mental note to make an appointment at Clip Rat's Salon and Day Spa.

I was still thinking about furcuts when the rodent suddenly tapped me on the forehead. He stared into my eyes.

CHEESE NIBLETS!

Was he trying to hypnotise me? I gulped. I'd read about bad mice like this. First they put you UNDER A SPELL. Then they break into your mouse hole and steal all your money!

The rodent's beady eyes seemed to drill right into me. I was so nervous I could barely see straight. I tried practising the deep-breathing techniques I had learned in Penny Pretzel Paw's yoga class. They didn't work. I guess I wasn't paying enough attention in class.

Just then, the rodent leaned in closer. I broke out in a cold sweat. "This is it," I mumbled to myself. **"Goodbye, cruel world."**

But instead of hypnotising me, the rodent snickered. "Don't you recognise me, Geronimo?" he said.

15

"It's **Kornelius von Kickpaw**."

I could hardly believe my eyes. The last time I'd seen Kornelius, I was still learning how to do maths and tie my shoes. **We were friends in primary school!**

A MOUSE WEARING A TRENCH COAT

In school, Kornelius sat at the desk behind me. He always wore a trench coat no matter what the weather was like. And he always wore dark sunglasses even when it wasn't sunny!

Yes, he was an odd sort of mouse, but we were good friends anyway. One time Wendell Wild Whiskers and his gang stuffed me into a locker. Kornelius came to my rescue. He ripped open the locker and made Wendell apologise. After that, the bullies never picked on me again. I always felt safe when Kornelius was around.

I smiled thinking about those days. Even though we hadn't squeaked in years, Kornelius would always be a great friend.

Do you have any friends like Kornelius? If you do,

you are very lucky. As my dear aunt Sweetfur likes to say, **"Whoever finds a friend ... finds a treasure!"**

I invited Kornelius into my house. Then I showed him around. It didn't take very long. My mouse hole isn't very big. Still, I'm super-proud of it. I especially love my kitchen with my mega-huge fridge.

While we were in the kitchen, I whipped up some tasty cheese on toast. Kornelius munched it down in two seconds flat! **Did I mention he's a big mouse?**

Finally, we sat down in my living room to chat. We had

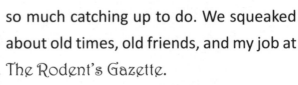

so much catching up to do. We squeaked about old times, old friends, and my job at The Rodent's Gazette.

"So what kind of work do you do,

Kornelius?" I asked.

My friend held up his paw.

"It's **TOP SECRET**," he whispered. "You have to promise you won't tell anyone."

I gasped. Why was my friend being so *mysterious*? Was he a professional burglar? Was he in the witmouse protection programme?

"I promise," I agreed, eyes wide.

Kornelius put his paws around my shoulder. Then he leaned in close and whispered, **"My code name is OOK. I'm a secret agent."**

VK
THE VON KICKPAW ESTATE

I was convinced Kornelius was **PULLING MY PAW**. I mean, I'd seen secret agents before in the movies, but not in New Mouse City.

"I'm not acting, Geronimo," my friend insisted. He drove me to his mansion in the country. On the way there, Kornelius explained that he was involved with secret missions for the government of Mouse Island. **I felt like I was in a dream.**

At last, we reached the mansion.

What a sight!

I knew my friend was rich, but this place was more spectacular than Elvis Mousely's estate! The property was surrounded by a gleaming wrought-iron gate with the letters VK inscribed at the entrance. The driveway wound its way past a perfectly manicured lawn.

1. Mansion
2. Greenhouse for rare plants
3. Tennis court
4. Helicopter pad
5. Garage
6. Swimming pool
7. Stable and paddock for horses
8. Private beach and yacht
9. Golf course

I spotted a greenhouse, tennis courts, and a stable for horses.

The inside of the mansion was almost as amazing as the outside. The entrance was made of white marble. Two magnificent gold and DIAMOND-STUDDED chandeliers glimmered over our heads. And there was even a fountain shaped like a gigantic wedge of cheese in the hallway. Kornelius ushered me into the living room. It was filled with priceless antiques. Paintings by famouse artists decorated the walls. I stared at a painting of a gorgeous rodent hanging above the fireplace.

Wow, what a *stunning* mouse! I couldn't take my eyes off her.

"That's my sister, Veronica," said Kornelius. "She's a secret agent, too. Her code name is 00V."

Just then, I sensed something behind me. When I turned around, **my jaw dropped**. It was her! It was 00V! My heart began racing like a car at the Indy Mouse 500. Did I mention I get a little nervous around beautiful rodents?

26

"Is that you on the wall? Uh, er, in the frame? I mean, in the painting?" I babbled.

The rodent flashed me a tiny smile. **Or was it a smirk?** Then she vanished. A delicate perfume lingered in the room.

Wow, what a *stunning* mouse!

I wondered if I could ask her out for a cup of hot Cheddar sometime. Too bad she disappeared so quickly.

I was still dreaming about 00V when Kornelius led me into the library. We sat down on two comfy leather pawchairs.

Without a word, Kornelius patted the arm of his chair. Seconds later, the rug slid aside. We were sitting on top of a trapdoor! Before I could let out a squeak, I found myself zipping down a steep, dark tunnel.

"Tell me when it's over!" I cried.

OOK'S SECRET LAB

1. Trapdoor
2. Tunnel
3. Secret lab
4. Computer area
5. Mega-globe
6. Instruments for scientific analysis
7. Control stations for wind tunnels
8. Garage for OO-car, OO-motorbike, OO-plane, and other vehicles
9. Lift for the OO-vehicles
10. Secret exit for the OO-vehicles
11. Secret dock for OO-boats

I'm a Secret Agent ...

Minutes later, we landed in an elegant living room. We were still seated in our pawchairs, but now we were underground in a very mysterious place.

I pinched myself to make sure I wasn't dreaming. **YOUCH!** That hurt! I may not be a tough mouse, but I do have one painful pinch.

After I recovered, Kornelius, aka 00K, showed me all of his agent gear. This included a bow tie that turned into a rope, a ring filled with **SNEEZING POWDER**, and anti-gravity shoes.

I was impressed and a little bit scared. Just then, Kornelius looked at me with a piercing stare. I gulped. **Had I done something wrong already?**

"Let me tell you why you're here," Kornelius began. He opened a little black case and took out a stack of newspapers.

Bow tie, when loosened, becomes a rope

Night-vision goggles

Belt and harness for a quick getaway

Paw-watch with micro movie projector

Mobile phone and video camera

Lock-picking tools hidden in shoe

Anti-noise and anti-gravity shoes

Anti-cat signal (can pick up cats' whereabouts for more than two miles)

Anti-cat vest

Inflatable boat

Very pesky microfleas reserve

Ring with sneezing powder

Sleeping powder

Fountain pen with microphone and stink bombs

am3e8v3759fjdlafvmdhfoq45677xdqifphlktnru3945
lktnru3945etvu9654seu4gnwryr9dMTPSsmaeam3ehr
am3e8v3759fjdlafvmdhfoq45677xd5677 3945
ehr
3945
ehr

OOK

NAME: Kornelius
von Kickpaw

CODE NAME: OOK

PROFESSION: Secret
agent

WHO HE IS: Geronimo's
friend from
primary school

PECULIARITIES:
Always wears a trench
coat and sunglasses,
even at night!

oq45677xdqifphlktnru3945
lktnru3945etvu9654seu4gnwryr9dMTPSsmaeam3ehr
am3e8v3759fjdlafvmdhfoq45677xdqifphlktnru3945

9dMTPSsmaeroasjetietvu9654seu49gOwtbtdòw'3955
9gO...8.3759fjdladqifp'3955fvmdhfoq45677x
9dM
9gO
9dM
9g
9d
9g
9d
9

OOV

NAME: Veronica
von Kickpaw

CODE NAME: OOV

PROFESSION: Secret
agent

WHO SHE IS: Kornelius's
sister

PECULIARITIES:
Always wears a
mysterious, delicate,
and sophisticated
perfume that makes her
immediately identifiable
and ... fascinating!

i9gOwtbtdòw8v3759fjdladqi...
c9dMTPSsmaeroasjetietvu9654seu49gOwtbtdòw'3955
i9gOwtbtdòw8v3759fjdladqifp'3955fvmdhfoq45677x
c9dMTPSsmaeroasjetietvu9654seu49gOwtbtdòw'3955

To my surprise, the articles were all about me. There was even a colour photo of me in front of The Rodent's Gazette. I have to admit it wasn't a very good one. "Are my ears really that big?" I muttered.

Kornelius shook his head. "Forget about your ears, Geronimo; you have more important things to worry about," he advised. "By reading the paper, anybody can figure out where you live, where you work, where you go on holiday, who your friends are. **Your life's one open book!**

"This is dangerous, Geronimo," he continued. "If an evil rodent wanted to hurt you or play a mean trick on you, they would have no problem. It would be like taking cheese from a young mouselet. You need someone to protect you. And I'm here to say, I'm your mouse."

I felt flattered. I mean, it's not often that you have a secret agent friend who wants to be **your own furry bodyguard**. Still, I politely declined.

Kornelius tried to make a list of all the things that could get me in trouble, and when it was time to leave,

Kornelius made me promise I would call him if I ever got into any trouble.

I grinned.

Aunt Sweetfur sure was right. **A friend is a true treasure.**

Or you could get run over by a car …

Or you could get kidnapped by a really evil rodent …

Or you could fall into a mousehole …

Or you could be harassed by an annoying author …

Or you could be chased by a crowd of admirers …

WHAT A GREAT DAY!

The next morning, I woke up feeling extra happy. I had good friends, a good family, and a great life. I gobbled down my breakfast and **Practically skipped** out my door. A strong wind was blowing, but I wasn't going to let that get me down. I smiled, thinking about how I used to love flying kites when I was a tiny mouselet. The sun was shining so I decided to walk to work.

What a great day!

While I was walking I thought about my friend Kornelius. He really didn't need to worry about me. Today I was feeling more than double OK!

The wind was blowing hard when I reached my

office. I shut the door behind me and raced upstairs.

"Geronimo, don't forget that today there is an important meeting with the president of the NEW MOUSE CITY HISTORICAL SOCIETY and your grandfather," Priscilla Prettywhiskers reminded me.

Do you know Priscilla? She's one of the editors at The Rodent's Gazette.

Now I looked at her and frowned.

"Meeting?" I mumbled. "What meeting?"

Priscilla reminded me that the head of the Historical Society was coming to check out The Rodent's Gazette.

It seems they were doing research on the oldest buildings in the city. The *Gazette* was on the list. Rats! **How could I forget such an important meeting?** I threw open the door to my office. I had to get my notes ready for the meeting. If I wasn't prepared, Grandfather would have my tail!

I was so worried about Grandfather that, at first, I didn't notice anything different. Then it hit me. A cold gust of wind sent my whiskers whirling. **CHEESE NIBLETS!** The night before I had accidentally left my window wide open!

I watched in horror as the fierce wind picked up a large envelope with a red seal. The gust lifted the envelope off my desk and blew it straight out the window. With a squeak, I tried catching it, but I was too late. My snout smacked down hard on my desk. Youch! I wondered if I'd ever be able to sniff again.

As I rubbed my nose, I told myself not to panic. After all, as the publisher of a newspaper, I was always getting tons of nutty post. That envelope was probably from some wacky mouse wanting me to do a story on ALIEN CATS or something.

I had forgotten to close the window … and there was a draught.

A gust of wind blew the envelope off my desk.

I THINK I LOST IT

At that moment, the door to my office burst open.

"Grandson! The meeting has already started! What are you doing in here?!" a gruff mouse shrieked.

I gulped. It was my highly stressed, highly irritable, highly demanding grandfather, William Shortpaws.

A shiver ran down my fur.

"The meeting has started. You're late, late, late, with a capital L!" he screamed. "The president of the NEW MOUSE CITY HISTORICAL SOCIETY and the committee members are waiting for us. Let's move it. And, Grandson, try not to embarrass me. Got it?"

We sat at our usual seats in the conference room.

Richard F. Ramblesnout, the head of the Historical Society, cleared his throat.

"Ahem, welcome, gentlemice. Let's get started. I'll be brief ...' he began.

I chewed my whiskers. Whenever anyone starts with "I'll be brief", they usually end up squeaking on and on forever. In fact, that's exactly what happened.

SNORE ...

After a little while, I began to doze off.

I was awakened by a piercing shout.

EEEH?

"Grandson!" yelled my grandfather. "Are you sleeping?"

My fur turned red with embarrassment.

WHO? ME?

"Did you hear what Mr. Ramblesnout said?" he shrieked. "There is an incredibly rare and valuable document on your desk. It's in a large envelope with a red seal on it. Go get it. Now!"

I couldn't move. I couldn't breathe. I couldn't think. How could this be happening? That envelope with the red seal on it was no junk mail. It was valuable. **Very valuable!**

DISBELIEF!

SYMPATHY!

ASTONISHMENT!

INDIGNATION!

BEWILDERMENT!

BAFFLEMENT!

ANNOYANCE!

ANGER!

SHOCK!

PITY!

"Um, well, unfortunately, I, um, think I lost it," I whispered softly.

Grandfather threw a fit.

"What?! Get that wax out of your ears and listen up. I want that document here, on this table, by nine o'clock tomorrow morning! Got it?" he shouted.

Everybody turned to look at me.

I felt faint.

I saw in their eyes: disbelief, shock, astonishment, bewilderment, bafflement, annoyance, indignation, anger, sympathy, and pity.

What could I do? What could I say? I had to find that envelope. I just had to!

"I'll do my best," I coughed.

Then I slunk out of the room with my tail between my legs.

50

A Volcano Ready to Explode

I got back to my office and collapsed behind my desk. **Oh, how did I get myself into such a mess?** I stared out the window. I could hear the wind roaring. It looked like a storm was brewing.

A few minutes later, Grandfather William scampered into my office.

He didn't slam the door. **Odd.**

He didn't yell. **Even more odd.**

I braced myself. Talk about a storm brewing. I knew Grandfather William too well. When he was angry, he was like a volcano ready to **EXPLODE**. Like a water balloon ready to pop. Like a pan of cheese popcorn ready to burst. Hmm … cheese popcorn … My stomach began to growl. I was hungry for my morning Cheddar muffin. But it would have to wait.

"Geronimo, do you have any idea what's inside that envelope?" he began.

I started to answer, but he interrupted me.

"It's the deed to this land!" he thundered. "It's the only proof we have that we own the property. If some rotten mouse gets his or her paws on that envelope, we'll lose *The Rodent's Gazette*!"

I closed my eyes. Oh, how did I get myself into such a mess?

I'm not sure I want to know!

How Hard Could It Be?

After Grandfather stormed out of my office, I had a terrible nightmare. Well, it wasn't exactly a nightmare since it was only eleven-thirty in the morning, but you get the idea. A **HORRIFYING** picture of Sally Ratmousen flashed before my eyes. She was waving an envelope with a red seal screaming, "The Rodent's Gazette is mine, mine, mine!"

I felt awful. Like I had just lost everything: the newspaper, my job, my appetite. Well, maybe not that last one. After all, it was nearly lunchtime.

Just then, I noticed a photo of me on my desk. It was a shot of me climbing Mouse Everest.

Suddenly, I felt a surge of energy. If I could climb a mountain as high as **Mouse Everest**, how hard could it be to find a silly old envelope?

By now it was noon. I needed to find the envelope by nine the next morning. That meant I still had twenty-one hours.

I grabbed a pen and paper and sat down to make a list. I love making lists. They help me to stay organised. I wrote down all of the things I needed to do:

1. Be calm.
2. Ask friends for help.
3. Call the weathermouse to find out the speed and direction of the wind.
4. Trace a possible route that the envelope might have taken on a map of New Mouse City.
5. Get going!

IMPORTANT!
Remember to take a supply of Cheesy Chews!

I began to do the things written on my list: 1. Be calm.

Then I called my sister Thea. The answering machine picked up.

"I'm not at home. Leave a message. *Beep!*"

I called my cousin Trap. His answering machine picked up, too.

"I'm not home. Or if I am, I'm busy eating. I mean, cooking. I mean eating and cooking. Leave a message. *Beep!*"

I thought about calling my friend Petunia Pretty Paws. She's so smart and beautiful. But I was too embarrassed. I didn't want Petunia to think I was a complete furbrain for losing such an important document. Instead, I tried my friend **Burt Burlyrat**. We had met at a survival camp in the jungle.

I got his answering machine. "I'm not in, but you might be able to find me in the Amazon. That is, if you don't mind a few hungry pythons and some killer quicksand. *Beep!*"

Why, oh, why, was no one home when I needed them?

For a nanosecond, I thought of OOK.

But just like with Petunia, I was too embarrassed. Besides, I had already told Kornelius I didn't need his help.

"All right, don't panic," I said out loud, trying to give myself a pep talk. "This means you will have no help. You will be all alone. And you will have to do everything yourself."

I put my head in my paws. Then I began sobbing uncontrollably.

Guess my pep talk needed work. Lots of work.

I began to do the things written on my list. 1. Be calm.

Why, oh, why, was no one home when I needed them?

You will be all alone. You will have to do everything by yourself.

I'm Your Biggest Fan!

After I stopped crying, I wrung out my whiskers. Then I looked at my list again.

I skipped over number one (Be calm), skipped number two (Ask friends for help), and went straight to numbers three and four. First I found a map of New Mouse City. I spread it out across my desk. Next I dialled the number for the local weather centre.

"Ahem, good morning. My name is Stilton, *Geronimo Stilton*. I need some information on the speed and direction of the wind in New Mouse City from around nine o'clock to twelve o'clock ..." I began.

I was greeted by an excited squeak.

1. Be calm.
2. Ask friends for help.
3. Call the weathermouse to find out the speed and direction of the wind.
4. Trace a possible route that the envelope might have taken on a map of New Mouse City.
5. Get going!
   IMPORTANT!
Remember to take a supply of Cheesy Chews!

58

"Oh, Mr. Stilton! What an honour! I am your **biggest fan**! I've read all of your books!" a female rodent gushed. "Why do you need to know about the wind? Are you writing a book about it? Are you coming down to the weather centre? Oh, I'm so **EXCiTED**. I would love to meet you. Maybe we can chat. Or do lunch. Or how about a movie?"

I blushed. Sometimes I'm a little shy around my female fans.

"Um, well, I don't have time to

come there today," I explained. "I really just need to know the direction of the wind."

"Of course, of course," the mouse agreed. Then she told me the **AWFUL NEWS**. It seemed the wind had done something really strange this morning. It had changed direction every fifteen minutes! She fired off a list of speeds and times.

By the time I got off the phone, my left ear was on fire, my paws were cramped, and I had made a date to go and see **THE RETURN OF CATZILLA**.

Oh, why could I never say no to my female fans?

HERE'S THE ROUTE
THE ENVELOPE TOOK

HOW EMBARRASSING!

Just then, I glanced at the clock. **CHEESE NIBLETS!** It was already 2:30 p.m. There was no time to waste.

14:30

I skipped straight to number five on my list: Get going! With a squeak, I scurried outside as fast as my paws would carry me.

I decided to check out New Mouse City's port. It's a very busy place. It's where all of the big boats enter the city dock. Plus, there are tons of vendors selling fresh fish, fruit, and vegetables.

By the time I reached the port, my paws were

throbbing. **Did I mention I'm not a very athletic mouse?** Still, there was no time to rest. I had to find that envelope! I scoured every fishing boat. I patted down every fishing net. I even peered in the open mouths of one hundred slimy tuna fish.

WHAT A STENCH! I could barely breathe. But I had to keep going.

Then I spotted a row of rubbish bins. Each one was filled with ROTTING, SMELLY FISH BONES.

What could I do? With a groan, I stuck my snout inside the first rubbish bin.

I didn't notice a woman staring at me.

"Aren't you Geronimo Stilton?" she said, wrinkling her nose.

It was Petunia Pretty Paws's aunt. How embarrassing!

A few minutes later, a very old mouse with a cane strolled by.

"Aren't you Geronimo Stilton?" he said, shaking his head.

It was my grandfather's old friend Sniffty. How embarrassing!

I stuck my snout deeper into the next rubbish bin, trying to hide. But a pretty young rodent spotted me.

"Aren't you Geronimo Stilton?" she said, looking shocked.

It was Benjamin's schoolteacher. How embarrassing!

I had made a fool of myself. And I hadn't even found the envelope! Two minutes later, a seagull swooped down and pooed right on my head. **What next?**

I CHECKED INSIDE RUBBISH BINS FILLED WITH STINKY FISH BONES.

ON TOP OF A STINKY MOUNTAIN

I sat on the pavement feeling totally depressed.
Just then, I heard a loud grumbling. My fur stood
on end. Was it a killer whale? Was it a ferocious sea
monster? Was this how it would all end? Headlines
flashed through my brain: CRAZED WHALE GRABS
STILTON BY THE TAIL! STILTON SUCKED
UP BY SEA CREATURE!

Then I realised the grumbling was coming from my tummy. I was starved!

Too bad I had forgotten the most important thing on my list: a supply of Cheesy Chews.

I stared at the SMELLY RUBBISH BINS, feeling even more depressed. And that's when it hit me. No, not more seagull poo. This time, it was an idea.

1. Be calm.
2. Ask friends for help.
3. Call the weathermouse to find out the speed and direction of the wind.
4. Trace a possible route that the envelope might have taken on a map of New Mouse City.
5. Get going!
IMPORTANT!
Remember to take a supply of Cheesy Chews!

Where could I find all the rubbish in New Mouse City? At the town dump, of course! If the envelope had fallen on the ground, it would surely have been swept up. Then it would go straight to the dump!

Right at that moment, a rubbish truck rumbled by. I took off like LIGHTNING. Like a rocket. Like the world's fastest marathon mouse. Well, okay, maybe I wasn't that fast. In fact, I was pretty slow. But don't tell anyone.

Before long, I reached the rubbish dump. **What a sight!** The rubbish was piled up a mile high. And it smelled worse than my cousin Rancid Rat's stinky breath. **I climbed on top of a huge pile and rested.**

Before throwing anything away, do you ever ask yourself if somebody else could use it, or if it could be recycled – that is, used again?

Certain types of rubbish, such as paper, plastic, glass, and aluminium are recyclable and can be used to produce new things. By recycling, we save natural resources and the energy that is needed to make new products.

Separating the recyclables
If we learn to divide rubbish according to its composition and place it in assigned containers, the paper, plastic, glass, and aluminium can be recycled.

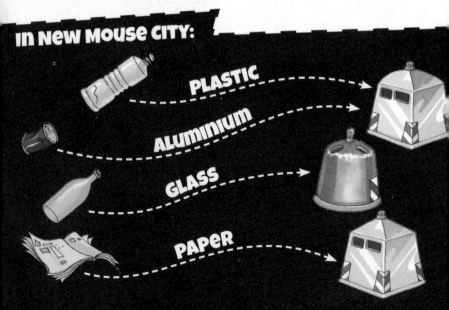

IN NEW MOUSE CITY:

PLASTIC

ALUMINIUM

GLASS

PAPER

RECYCLING PLANTS

There are recycling centres that collect various types of rubbish, such as paper, glass, plastic, and aluminium, rework it, and then reuse it.

RUBBISH DUMPS

All rubbish that is not recyclable ends up in rubbish dumps.

INCINERATORS

There are plants where rubbish is burned to eliminate it. As the refuse is burned, a tremendous amount of heat is released, which can then be transformed into energy.

What can YOU do?

Squash plastic bottles and place them in the appropriate containers.

Pick up all papers, newspapers, magazines, and cardboard, tie them in bundles and recycle them.

Use your imagination to reuse things you thought you no longer needed.

For example, you can change an empty ice cream plastic container into a delightful boat. Try to figure out how!

Before buying a new thing, stop and think: do I really need it?

RUBBISH, MORE RUBBISH, AND ... EVEN MORE RUBBISH!

Just then a truck arrived. And before I could squeak, it happened. A whole mound of new rubbish came pouring out of the truck. It all crashed down right on top of me! I began rolling down the hill like an out-of-control furball. **Oh, what a mess I was in this time.** And I mean *mess*! I tried to grab hold of something, but all I got was a rotten banana peel. "Help!" I screeched. **"I'M BEING BURIED ALIVE IN JUNK!"**

Suddenly, I felt two strong paws pulling me out of the rubbish heap.

"I'm here to help," a deep voice said. At the same time, I smelled a *delicate perfume*.

Hmm ... it seemed so familiar.

"Thanks," I mumbled before I passed out.

When I came to, I was still at the town dump, but I wasn't rolling anymore. I looked around. I was alone.

Who had saved me?

And why did he disappear?

It was a real mystery.

I was still thinking about my mysterious rescuer when I noticed the wind had picked up. Thousands of pieces of paper began swirling all around me.

At that moment, I spotted an envelope drifting right above my head.

Could it be? **IT WAS!** It was the envelope with the red seal – the one I'd been searching for!

But just as I reached to grab it, it disappeared down a mousehole cover.

DOWN, DOWN, DOWN ... INTO A SEA OF FOUL SLIME

What could I do? I had to get that envelope.

With a groan, I lifted up the grate and lowered myself into the mousehole. It was dark. So very dark. My teeth began to chatter. **Did I mention I'm afraid of the dark, and tight spaces, and the ding of the toaster oven?**

Oh, but that's another story for another time. I was wishing I had worn the **glow-in-the-dark tie** my cousin Trap had given me so I could see a little better. Just then, I slipped.

Down, down, down I tumbled, snoutfirst into the darkness.

After what seemed like a million years, I landed with a **SICKENING SPLASH**. I found myself floating in a sea of slimy green liquid. The smell was worse than the town dump. Welcome to the sewers of New Mouse City.

I dragged myself out of the water and looked around. No sign of the envelope with the red seal.

But I did see something. Something shiny and yellow. I blinked. A pair of glittering eyes stared at me through the darkness.

My whiskers began to tremble. Who in their right mind would live down here in the SEWER?

Just then, the creature cackled softly. "Ha, ha, ha." Was it laughing at me? Was it going to pounce on me? Was this how it would all end?

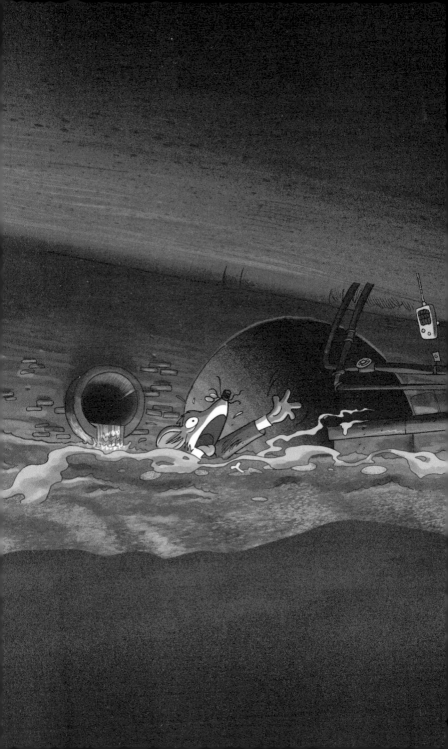

I braced myself for an attack, but nothing happened. Instead, the yellow eyes took off into the darkness. At first, I was glad to see them go. Then I was even more scared. Without those eyes, the sewer was darker than theatre four at the Cheddarville Tenplex. There was only one thing left to do. **Follow those eyes.**

I chased them the entire night. I was exhausted. Finally, they stopped, turned around, and started chasing me!

RANCID RAT HAIRS! Now what was I supposed to do?

"Ha, ha, ha," the creature cackled.

This was it. I was a goner. Oh, why hadn't I let my friend Kornelius help me? He was right. I was no good at protecting myself. I was always getting myself into these jams. I mean, the last time I tried to bake cookies I got my tail stuck in the oven. My **BURNING FUR** set off the smoke alarm. I was so embarrassed when the firemice showed up on my doorstep.

"HELP! HELP! SOMEBODY HELP ME!" I squeaked at the top of my lungs.

Meanwhile, the yellow eyes zoomed closer.

Suddenly, I realised who they belonged to: an enormous crocodile! And even worse, it was holding the envelope with the red seal in its **FEROCIOUS JAWS**!

CHEESE NIBLETS! I closed my eyes and wished for a miracle. I could hear the crocodile gnashing its teeth. Its breath smelled like rotten goat's cheese. Hadn't this guy heard about the dangers of tooth decay?

I was still thinking about teeth when someone grabbed me by the shoulder.

"I'm here to help," a familiar voice said. Again, I smelled a *delicate perfume*.

I opened my eyes, but it was too dark. I could only

see the eyes of the crocodile. They were staring right at me. The croc looked hungry. **VERY HUNGRY.**

"Goodbye, cruel world," I sobbed. Then I fainted.

When I came to, I was back on the street. It was already dawn.

I looked all around me but didn't see anyone.

Who had saved me?

Why did he disappear?

It was a real mystery.

UP, UP, UP ... INTO SALLY RATMOUSEN'S OFFICE

I sat on the curb feeling totally confused.

What had just happened to me?

How did I get out of the sewer?

Who was my *mysterious rescuer*?

But above all, what happened to the envelope with the red seal that was between the crocodile's teeth?

Do you know what happened next? **A miracle.** A real miracle. I looked up and there it was – the envelope! The wind had picked it up and carried it high above my head.

It flew higher and higher.

An instant later, it slipped into an open window.

DOUBLE-TWISTED RATTAILS! That window

belonged to my biggest enemy, Sally Ratmousen. Do you know Sally? She is the owner of **The Daily Rat**. Her dream is to put The Rodent's Gazette out of business.

Now what was I supposed to do? Sally would never let me into her office. Firstly, I was covered in STINKY SMELLY SLIME from the sewer. And secondly, Sally hated me!

I glanced at my watch. It was 8:30 a.m. Yikes! Only thirty minutes left!

That's it, I decided. I had no choice.

I'm going in. I slunk up the steps of **The Daily Rat** and squeezed through the doors. I did it! I was in! I was so proud of myself I barely noticed where I was going. Before I knew it, I was standing right outside Sally's office.

I peeked inside. Sally was seated behind her huge crystal desk. The desk was empty except for one thing. I gulped. It was the envelope. The envelope with the red seal.

I was just about to dash in and grab it when Sally spotted me. Or should I say SMELLED me.

"Geronimo Stilton!" she screeched. "What are you doing here in my office? You smell worse than the inside of the Cheddartown stables." Just then, she realised I was staring at the envelope.

"Hmm, I see I have something you want," she cackled. She picked up the envelope and fanned her snout. "I don't know what it is, but **it's mine, mine, mine**!"

I groaned. I should have known Sally would never give up without a fight. I tried every trick in the book.

"FIRE! ALIENS! RUN FOR YOUR LIFE!" I squeaked. But Sally didn't budge.

Then I had an idea. "Sally, I hate to alarm you," I whispered. "But you broke a pawnail."

That did it. Sally flew into a frenzy. "Where, where?" she shrieked.

In a flash, I grabbed the envelope. I raced for the door.

But I wasn't fast enough. Sally grabbed me by the tail. The envelope flew out of my paws. I watched in horror as it drifted out the window.

I felt my heart sink. This was it. I'd never find that envelope again. I was a dead rat. And maybe sooner than I thought. Sally's muscular bodyguard was staring at me like I was a piping-hot three-cheese pizza!

"Musclerat, please take Mr. Stilton away. And make sure you teach him a lesson he'll never forget," she ordered with an evil smirk.

Musclerat lifted me into the air with one paw. **HOLEY CHEESE, THAT RODENT WAS STRONG!** I mean, I'm not the heaviest mouse in the world, but I'm no lightweight. Plus, I have to admit lately I'd been cheating on my diet.

Musclerat carried me down the hall. Then he locked me inside the broom cupboard.

"I heard you liked dark places," he snickered.

I felt dizzy. My paws started to sweat. My heart

started to pound. I began to sob uncontrollably. "Somebody help me," I wailed.

Suddenly, I heard a *click* and the door opened. I felt someone grab my shoulder.

A deep voice said, *"I'm here to help."*

The same *delicate perfume* I had smelled before filled my nose.

I tried to say thanks, but I couldn't.

I had fainted.

89

THE CASE OF THE MYSTERIOUS RESCUER

When I came to, I found myself outside. I was sitting on the pavement in front of **The Daily Rat**. It was 8:45 a.m. I looked all around me, but I didn't see anyone.

Who had saved me?

Why did he disappear?

I felt like I was on one of those true-life mystery shows on TV: The Case of the Mysterious Rescuer. Too bad everything wasn't going to work out perfectly in the end. I still hadn't found the lost envelope with the red seal. I stared at the ground feeling glum.

Who had saved me and why?

My grandfather would never let me live this one down. I'd be **HUMILIATED** in front of all of my co-workers. I'd have to leave the *Gazette*. I'd

have no money, no job. I'd wander the streets looking for food. Well, at least I knew how to get to the town dump. Maybe I could find some scraps of **MOULDY CHEESE**.

A tear slid down my fur. Then another and another. Soon, I was bawling my eyes out. Just then I felt someone touch my shoulder. At the same time, I smelled that *perfume* again.

"I'm here to help," a deep voice said. And then it hit me. No, not more rubbish. Not more seagull poo. It hit me who the voice belonged to. I jumped off the curb and whirled around. **I WAS RIGHT!**

The voice belonged to my old friend Kornelius. Yep, I was snout to snout with 00K and the fascinating 00V!

"How can we help you?" they asked.

I let out a long sigh.

"I lost an envelope, a very important envelope," I moaned. **"And now my grandfather's going to kill me!"**

For some reason, Kornelius, aka 00K, and his sister Veronica, aka 00V, looked at each other and smiled.

"A large envelope?" said 00K.

"With a red seal?" said 00V.

My jaw hit the ground. These secret agents were unbelievable! I had no idea they were mind readers.

I nodded, awestruck. Then Kornelius handed me something. My eyes nearly popped out of my fur.

It was the envelope!

"But … how … when … what?" I spluttered.

Kornelius just grinned. "We secret agents work in mysterious ways," he said.

His sister 00V nodded.

I wondered if they could read my mind now. I was so happy. **I felt like I had just won a lifetime supply of Cheesy Chews!**

COUNTDOWN: FIVE, FOUR, THREE ...

Suddenly, I remembered the time. I glanced at my paw-watch. *HOLEY CHEDDAR CHUNKS!* It was 8:55 a.m.!

I only had five minutes to get the envelope to my grandfather.

I took off as fast as my paws could carry me. I was a mouse on a mission – a mission to save my tail! I flew up the steps to the *Gazette*, raced past my office, and headed straight for the conference room. By the time I reached the door, I was sweating like an overweight rat on a treadmill. **MY PAWS WERE ACHING.** And my heart was beating so hard, I thought it might pop right out of my fur.

I flung open the door to the conference room just as the clock chimed nine. I wasn't surprised to see my grandfather waiting for me.

Did I mention he's a stickler for punctuality?

"Here it is, Grandfather," I huffed, waving the envelope in the air. Then I collapsed in a heap.

"Well, well, well, Grandson. I wasn't sure you had it in you," my grandfather smirked. "But it looks like you passed my test WITH FLYING COLOURS. You see, Geronimo, the envelope you have contains a copy of the original document. I've had the original here with me this whole time. I just wanted to see how much The Rodent's Gazette meant to you. And now I can see it means a lot."

I didn't know whether to laugh or cry. But it didn't matter. **I had already fainted.**

A True Friend ...

They took me home on a stretcher.

I was exhausted. I slept all day and all night for twenty-four hours straight.

The next day, OOK came to see me at the office.

I told him how silly I felt.

"I should have admitted that I needed your help," I confessed. "But there's one thing I still don't understand. What made you follow me even after I told you I could take care of myself?"

Kornelius laughed. "We secret agents have a SIXTH SENSE, Geronimo." He winked. "Plus, you always had a knack for getting yourself into trouble when we were little. Remember the time you accidentally flew off that swing at break time?"

How could I forget? I got stuck in a HUMONGOUS THORNY BUSH. Youch! My fur hurt just thinking about it.

Before Kornelius left, he gave me a present. It was a special satellite phone to wear around my neck.

Now all I had to do was press a button to contact my friend.

I told you my aunt Sweetfur was right.

A FRIEND...

THE RODENT'S GAZETTE

1. Main entrance
2. Printing presses (where everything is printed)
3. Accounts department
4. Editorial room (where editors, illustrators, and designers work)
5. Geronimo Stilton's office
6. Geronimo's botanical garden

MAP OF NEW MOUSE CITY

1. Industrial Zone
2. Cheese Factories
3. Angorat International Airport
4. WRAT Radio and Television Station
5. Cheese Market
6. Fish Market
7. Town Hall
8. Snotnose Castle
9. The Seven Hills of Mouse Island
10. Mouse Central Station
11. Trade Centre
12. Movie Theatre
13. Gym
14. Catnegie Hall
15. Singing Stone Plaza
16. The Gouda Theatre
17. Grand Hotel
18. Mouse General Hospital
19. Botanical Gardens
20. Cheap Junk for Less (Trap's store)
21. Parking Lot
22. Mouseum of Modern Art
23. University and Library
24. The Daily Rat
25. The Rodent's Gazette
26. Trap's House
27. Fashion District
28. The Mouse House Restaurant
29. Environmental Protection Centre
30. Harbour Office
31. Mousidon Square Garden
32. Golf Course
33. Swimming Pool
34. Blushing Meadow Tennis Courts
35. Curlyfur Island Amusement Park
36. Geronimo's House
37. Historic District
38. Public Library
39. Shipyard
40. Thea's House
41. New Mouse Harbour
42. Luna Lighthouse
43. The Statue of Liberty
44. Hercule Poirat's Office
45. Petunia Pretty Paws's House
46. Grandfather William's House

MAP OF MOUSE ISLAND

1. Big Ice Lake
2. Frozen Fur Peak
3. Slipperyslopes Glacier
4. Coldcreeps Peak
5. Ratzikistan
6. Transratania
7. Mount Vamp
8. Roastedrat Volcano
9. Brimstone Lake
10. Poopedcat Pass
11. Stinko Peak
12. Dark Forest
13. Vain Vampires Valley
14. Goosebumps Gorge
15. The Shadow Line Pass
16. Penny-Pincher Castle
17. Nature Reserve Park
18. Las Ratayas Marinas
19. Fossil Forest
20. Lake Lake
21. Lake Lakelake
22. Lake Lakelakelake
23. Cheddar Crag
24. Cannycat Castle
25. Valley of the Giant Sequoia
26. Cheddar Springs
27. Sulphurous Swamp
28. Old Reliable Geyser
29. Vole Vale
30. Ravingrat Ravine
31. Gnat Marshes
32. Munster Highlands
33. Mousehara Desert
34. Oasis of the Sweaty Camel
35. Cabbagehead Hill
36. Rattytrap Jungle
37. Rio Mosquito
38. Mousefort Beach
39. San Mouscisco
40. Swissville
41. Cheddarton
42. Mouseport
43. New Mouse City
44. Pirate Ship of Cats

THE COLLECTION

HAVE YOU READ ALL OF GERONIMO'S ADVENTURES?

ABOUT THE AUTHOR

Born in New Mouse City, Mouse Island, GERONIMO STILTON is Rattus Emeritus of Mousomorphic Literature and of Neo-Ratonic Comparative Philosophy. For the past twenty years, he has been running The Rodent's Gazette, New Mouse City's most widely read daily newspaper.

Stilton was awarded the Ratitzer Prize for his scoops on *The Curse of the Cheese Pyramid* and *The Search for Sunken Treasure*. He has also received the Andersen Prize

for Personality of the Year. His works have been published all over the globe.

In his spare time, Mr. Stilton collects antique cheese rinds and plays golf. But what he most enjoys is telling stories to his nephew Benjamin.